DATE DUE

Passing the Music Down

PASSING THE MUSIC DOWN

Sarah Sullivan

illustrated by

Barry Root

CANDLEWICK PRESS

Come August, with corn strutting high in the fields
and tomatoes plumping out on the vine,
folks get to talking about tuning up and
heading over twisty mountain roads
to hear fiddle players and banjo pickers
make music under the stars.

They travel through the heartland,
past cold factories and drifty towns
to the old, old mountains
slumbering east of Tennessee.

Come to hear a man
bent by stooping in the mines,
come to hear him lift his bow
and set his spirit free.

"Play 'Liza Jane'!" shouts a boy
from the crowd.
Traveled clear from Indiana
just to hear that fiddler play.

With his hands gnarled from work,
the old man lifts his bow.
Gives a nod to the crowd
and saws out a lick.

Passing the music down.

"Play some more?" asks the boy.
Then he strides up front,
takes a seat beside the fiddler
on a tall wooden stool.

"Know any of my music?"
asks the old man.
The boy lifts his arm and
plays "Peg 'n' Awl,"
his chest near to bursting
with all that hope inside.

"That's pretty good,"
the old man says.
"You got to start with a spin
and end with a skid."

Like a katydid in spring,
the boy's heart dances.
"Will you teach me all your tunes?"
he asks with a gulp.
"Will you show me how they go?
I want to play like you."

The fiddler wipes his brow,
takes a long, slow look.
"You ought to bring that boy to see me,"
he tells the young man's folks.
"Pay a visit to the farm,
and we'll play some old-time tunes."

Passing the music down.

Rolling up the hollow
through the early morning mist,
the boy's father steers the car
around two friendly old hounds.

"Been wondering when you'd get here,"
the old man tells the boy.
"Got a lot of things to show you.
I hope you'll spend some time."

They flip flapjacks for breakfast.

They hunt ginseng in the woods.

They pick runners from the garden.

And, when the work is done,
they sit out on the porch.
The old man tunes his fiddle,
and the boy leans in close.

They play "Bonaparte's Retreat"
and "Yew Piney Mountain,"
tunes older than the towns
the boy traveled through,
tunes old as the mist
and twisty as the roads.

Passing the music down.

Soon the boy and his family
are putting down roots
in the next county over
from the old man's farm.
On cold December nights
they fiddle by the fire.
Snow settles deep against the fence, and
the boy settles deep inside the music.
The old man shares his stories.
They've become the best of friends.

When the creek swells in spring
and the rooster cock-a-doodles,
they gather fiddleheads for lunch
and mend fence posts by the well.

Seedlings dot the garden
when they fiddle down in Charleston.
Bees nuzzle honeysuckle
when they jam up at Glenville.
Frost stiffens hay bales
when they teach out at Elkins.
Their lives are stitched together
in a quilt of old-time tunes.

Passing the music down.

Charleston

Glenville

Elkins

Life scoots along.
The boy's back grows straight and tall.
The old man's knees turn wobbly.
He turned ninety a few years past.
Still he tends the garden
and plays music with the boy.

Until one cold frosty morning
just before spring,
the old man's legs won't move
the way they need to go.
He can't lift a log from
the woodpile to the fire.
Can't make the journey
from his kitchen to the porch.

Sitting at his bedside,
the boy holds his friend's hand,
hums a tune low and soft
all the way to the end.
Sees the old man smile
when he hears the boy's words.
"I'll do just like I promised.
I'll teach folks all your tunes.
There's a part of you that
will always be around."

Passing the music down.

Now the years have passed
since the old man taught the boy.
The young man plays his fiddle
at festivals and fairs.
"Play 'Liza Jane'!" shouts a boy
from the crowd.
Traveled quite a distance just to
hear that young man play.

The fiddler lifts his bow
and plays the old-time tune.
There's an echo in his heart
as he saws out a *rrrrip!*
He hears the old man's voice
in a memory deep inside.

Play that fiddle, son.
You got to pass the music down.

This book was inspired by the true story of two celebrated musicians, Melvin Wine and Jake Krack, who, despite an age difference of seventy-five years, performed fiddle music together and became the best of friends.

Melvin Wine was born and raised in Braxton County, West Virginia, where his father, grandfather, and great-grandfather had all been known as musicians. Melvin and his wife, Etta, had ten children. They lived on a farm where they raised cattle and cultivated a garden. To support his family, Melvin worked in and around the coal mines for thirty-seven years. He put his fiddle away while his children were young and did not play for nearly twenty years. After his children were grown, Melvin started playing again, and during the 1960s, he played in competitions and at the State Folk Festival in Glenville, West Virginia. Throughout the sixties and seventies, Melvin's participation in competitions and festivals increased, as the nation saw a revival of interest in traditional folk music. Melvin continued to play through the eighties and nineties and even into the twenty-first century. In 1991, he received a National Heritage Fellowship from the National Endowment for the Arts.

Jake Krack began hearing stories about Melvin Wine when he was a nine-year-old fiddle student in Indiana. At the urging of his teacher, a man named Brad Leftwich, Jake traveled with his parents to Clifftop, West Virginia, in the summer of 1995 to hear Melvin play at the Appalachian String Band Festival. Melvin was already eighty-six years old, and Jake was anxious to learn as much as he could while Melvin was still playing music.

Over the next two years, Jake and his parents made frequent trips to West Virginia so Jake could study with Melvin and learn his tunes and bowing techniques. Jake received support and encouragement from the Indiana Arts Commission and the Augusta Heritage Center of Davis and Elkins College.

Jake's parents were anxious to help him pursue his dream of learning to play old-time music. So in 1998, when Jake was thirteen, his mother, Dara, accepted a job as a school librarian in Charleston, West Virginia. By Thanksgiving of that year, Jake and his family were living on a farm in rural Calhoun County, about an hour's drive north of Charleston. While his friendship with Melvin grew, Jake also studied with other old-time musicians, including Lester McCumbers, Bobby Taylor, and Wilson Douglas. He had an apprenticeship with McCumbers through a program sponsored by the Augusta Heritage Center.

In 2000, Jake played on the Millennium Stage at the Kennedy Center in Washington, D.C. In 2002, seven years after meeting Melvin for the first time, Jake became the youngest musician to be named State Fiddle Champion in the under-sixty category at the annual Vandalia Gathering on the grounds of the West Virginia state capitol. Upon graduating from high school in 2003, Jake enrolled at Berea College, in Kentucky, where he earned a degree in Appalachian studies. During his years at Berea, Jake worked in the college library. Part of his job there was to archive recordings of traditional music, including recordings by his mentors, Melvin Wine and Lester McCumbers.

In 2006, Jake won first place in the old-time fiddlers' contest at Clifftop, the place where he had first met Melvin in 1995. Jake knows it is up to him to pass on the music he has learned from the old masters. "It's a promise that I made to Lester and Melvin," he says, "that I'd play the songs just like they do, as a way of preserving the music."

Melvin Wine died in 2003 at the age of ninety-three. His music lives on in the recordings he left behind and in the students whose lives he touched, especially Jake Krack, who plays Melvin's tunes and continues the tradition of passing the music down.

═══ A NOTE ON THE TUNES ═══

"Peg 'n' Awl" was the tune Jake played for Melvin when they first met at Clifftop in 1995. Jake had learned it when Brad Leftwich gave him a recording of Melvin playing that tune. "Peg 'n' Awl," "Bonaparte's Retreat," "Cold Frosty Morning," "Liza Jane," and "Yew Piney Mountain" were all part of Melvin Wine's repertoire. "Yew Piney Mountain" is what is known as a "crooked tune," meaning that it does not follow traditional meter and rhythmic patterns.

RESOURCES

♪ Books and Articles

Beisswenger, Drew. *Fiddling Way Out Yonder: The Life and Music of Melvin Wine.* Jackson: University Press of Mississippi, 2002.

Clines, Francis X. "Passing Along the Art of Appalachian Fiddling." *New York Times,* October 10, 1999, sec. 1.

Hafenbrack, Josh. "Music for the Soul." *Charleston Daily Mail,* May 23, 2002, D1.

Hayes, John. "In a West Virginia Hollow, Mountain Music Thrives." *Post-Gazette,* August 17, 2003. http://www.post-gazette/ae/200308177fiddle0817fnp2.asp.

Leffler, Susan. "Melvin Wine." *Mountains of Music: West Virginia Traditional Music from Goldenseal,* edited by John Lilly, 7–11. Chicago University of Illinois Press, 1999.

Lowe, Jared. "Fancy fingerwork." *Charleston Gazette,* March 11, 2000, C2.

Marshall, Erynn. *Music in the Air Somewhere.* Morgantown: West Virginia University Press, 2006.

Milnes, Gerald. *Play of a Fiddle: Traditional Music, Dance, and Folklore in West Virginia.* Lexington: University Press of Kentucky, 1999.

Orosz, Monica. "He's Fiddling with Tradition." *Charleston Daily Mail,* February 24, 2000, 1.

♪ Discography

Jake Krack. *Home At Last.* WiseKrack Records, 2000.

———. *Hope I'll Join the Band.* WISE-1702, WiseKrack Records, 2002.

———. *How 'bout That.* WiseKrack Records, 1997.

———. *One More Time.* WiseKrack Records, 1998.

———. *Second Time Around.* WISE-1904, WiseKrack Records, 2005.

———. *Wire Fire.* WiseKrack Records, 2001.

——— and Doug Van Gundy. *Two Far Gone.* WiseKrack Records, 1999.

Melvin Wine. *Hannah at the Springhouse.* AHS-2, Marimac, 1999.

——— and various artists. *Classic Old-Time Fiddle from Smithsonian Folkways.* Smithsonian Folkways Recordings, 2007.

♪ Videos

Fiddles, Snakes, and Dog Days: Old-Time Music and Lore in West Virginia. Elkins, WV: Augusta Heritage Center, 1997.

Old Time Music Maker: Melvin Wine. Glen Arbor, MI: Communicraft Productions, 1993.

Soundmix: Five Young Musicians. Free Range Productions, 2004.

♪ Websites

www.augustaheritage.com	August Heritage Center of Davis and Elkins College
www.folkways.si.edu	Smithsonian Folkways
www.jakekrack.com	Jake Krack's website
www.loc.gov/folklife	The American Folklife Center
www.wvculture.org	West Virginia Division of Culture and History

In memory of Melvin Wine

Thanks to everyone at Vermont College, the West Virginia Arts Commission,
Jake, Dara, and Reed Krack; Barry Root, Hilary Breed Van Dusen, and Sara Busse;
special thanks to Leda Schubert for invaluable insight and support,
and most of all, to my husband, Rick.

S. S.

Text copyright © 2010 by Sarah Sullivan
Illustrations copyright © 2010 by Barry Root

First edition 2011

Library of Congress Cataloging-in-Publication Data

Sullivan, Sarah.
Passing the music down / Sarah Sullivan ; illustrated by Barry Root. —1st ed.
p. cm.
Summary: A boy and his family befriend a country fiddler, who teaches the boy all about playing
the old tunes, which the boy promised to help keep alive. Inspired by Melvin Wine and Jake Krack.
ISBN 978-0-7636-3753-8
[1. Fiddlers—Fiction. 2. Folk music—Fiction. 3. Country life—Fiction.]
I. Root, Barry, ill. II. Title.
PZ7.S95355Pas 2010
[E]—dc22   2008037104

11 12 13 14 15 16 SCP 10 9 8 7 6 5 4 3 2 1

Printed in Humen, Dongguan, China

This book was typeset in Gothic Blonde.
The illustrations were done in watercolor and gouache.

Candlewick Press
99 Dover Street
Somerville, Massachusetts 02144

visit us at www.candlewick.com